Special thanks to Liss Norton

For Arabella Shepperd,
who'd love to visit
the Fairy Fairground!
With love. XXX

ORCHARD BOOKS
338 Euston Road, London NW1 3BH
Orchard Books Australia
Level 17/207 Kent Street, Sydney, NSW 2000
A Paperback Original

First published in 2015 by Orchard Books

Text © Hothouse Fiction Limited 2015

Illustrations © Orchard Books 2015

A CIP catalogue record for this book is available
from the British Library.

ISBN 978 1 40833 305 1

1 3 5 7 9 10 8 6 4 2

Printed in Great Britain

MIX
Paper from
responsible sources
FSC® C104740

The paper and board used in this book are made from wood from responsible sources.

Orchard Books is an imprint of Hachette Children's Books and published by
The Watts Publishing Group Limited, an Hachette UK company

www.hachette.co.uk

Series created by Hothouse Fiction
www.hothousefiction.com

Twinkle Trophy

ROSIE BANKS

ORCHARD

Fairy
Fairground

Contents

A Place of Magical Fun

"I want to try the hoopla," said Ellie Macdonald excitedly. "One of the prizes is an art set!" Ellie and her best friends, Summer Hammond and Jasmine Smith, were at the Honeyvale County Fair. Ellie's parents and her little sister, Molly, were there too, but they'd let Summer, Jasmine and Ellie go off by themselves to explore the stalls and to look at the farm

animals. The girls were having a brilliant
time!

"I'd like to win that cute toy lamb,"
Summer said as she looked at the hoopla
prizes. "The real ones over there were so
sweet!"

They gave their money to the lady
running the stall and took three hoops
each. Ellie aimed at the art set, but two
of her hoops sailed past it and the third
fell short.

"Bad luck," said Jasmine. "I'll see if
I can win it for you!" But her hoops
missed as well.

"My turn," said Summer. She stared at
the toy lamb hopefully, trying to judge
the distance, then threw her first hoop.
It brushed the lamb's ears, but it didn't
go over the toy. Her second two hoops

missed the lamb, but she did ring a pack of three fancy chocolates.

"Well done!" Jasmine exclaimed.

Summer shared out the sweets. "Come on," she said as they munched happily, "Let's see what else there is to do!"

"What's that over there?" Ellie asked,

spotting a white tent with a colourful flag fluttering above it.

"It's a magic show," Jasmine said. "I saw a poster earlier."

"Let's go and watch!" Ellie suggested.

The girls headed for the tent. Lots of people were already inside. The youngest children were sitting on the ground near the stage, while older children and grown-ups were on chairs behind them. The girls found three seats at the back.

The magician was wearing a black cloak with a shiny red lining, white gloves and a black top hat.

"Welcome, ladies and gentlemen, boy and girls," he said. "Prepare to be amazed by my magic tricks!" Taking off his hat, he showed everyone that it was empty. Then he put it on a table

and tapped it with his magic wand.
"Abracadabra," he cried, and pulled out
a bunch of fake flowers. The audience
clapped.

"It's fun, but it's not the same as the
real magic that happens in the Secret

Kingdom," whispered Ellie.

Jasmine and Summer nodded in
agreement.

The girls shared an amazing secret.
They had a magic box that could
take them to a place called the Secret
Kingdom – a beautiful land full of pixies,
elves, unicorns and all kinds of other
amazing creatures.

The box had been made by kind King
Merry, the ruler of the kingdom, because
the magical land was in danger from his
mean sister Queen Malice – and Ellie,
Summer and Jasmine were the only
people who could help!

"This magic show is making me
think about Trixi," whispered Summer.
Trixibelle was their pixie friend, and
King Merry's assistant. She and the girls

had been tricked by Queen Malice into wearing cursed friendship bracelets that had stolen their special talents. Luckily it was Talent Week in the Secret Kingdom, and once the prizes had been presented, the winners could use the awards' magic to restore the girls' special gifts.

Ellie's art skills, Jasmine's talent for music and dancing, and Summer's ability to befriend animals had all been returned already. But poor Trixi's talent for magic was still missing, and the girls could hardly wait to go to the Secret Kingdom to help her get it back.

"We have to break Queen Malice's spell before Talent Week is over," said Jasmine in a low voice. "Otherwise Trixi will never be able to use magic again!"

"But we can't go until we get a

message from her," Summer whispered. She hoped they'd hear from their pixie friend very soon.

The magician placed a yellow hanky in his hat. When he pulled it out again it had turned red. The audience clapped, but the girls sighed.

Then suddenly, Ellie noticed light coming from Jasmine's bag. "The Magic Box," she whispered excitedly, nudging her friends. Jasmine pulled the bag out from under her chair and they hurried out of the tent and hid behind a nearby tree.

Sure enough, the curved mirror on the top was shining brightly. As they peered at it, words began to appear there. Summer read them out:

"Come to a place of fairy fun!
Come one, come all, come everyone!
With games and stalls and treats and slides,
Come to the place with magic rides!"

The box lid flew open and the map of the Secret Kingdom floated out. Ellie grabbed it and spread it out on the grass between them. "We're looking for a place full of *fairy fun*," she muttered.

They all bent low over the map. "But

everywhere in the Secret Kingdom is full of fun!" said Jasmine.

"Except Thunder Castle," said Summer

with a shiver. "There's no fun where Queen Malice lives!"

"It's somewhere there are *magic rides*,"

Jasmine said. She spotted Unicorn Valley on the map, where two beautiful white unicorns were cantering down a hill. "You can ride unicorns in Unicorn Valley, but I don't think there are any slides there…"

"What about this place?" said Ellie. She pointed to a fairground near the bottom of the map. Tiny figures were flitting around a Ferris wheel and a tall rollercoaster. "There are loads of rides."

Jasmine peered more closely. "It's called the Fairy Fairground," she said, reading the tiny writing. "A place of fairy fun! That must be it!"

Excitedly the girls placed their hands over the six green gems that surrounded the mirror. "The answer is the Fairy Fairground," they cried together.

Golden sparkles
began to pour
out of the
magic box.
Suddenly
they heard
a voice
calling from
somewhere
above their
heads: "Oh
dearie, dearie me!
Help!"

The girls looked up in surprise, and saw
an anxious face peeping down
at them from the branches of the tree.

"It's King Merry!" said Summer in
astonishment.

"Are you OK, Your Majesty?" Ellie

called up to him.

"Where's Trixi?" Jasmine asked.

"Oh dearie me, thank goodness I've found you, girls!" King Merry cried. "Something terrible has happened – Trixi is missing!"

The Fairy Fairground

"Hold on, Your Majesty," Jasmine said.
She scrambled onto a low branch, then
pulled herself up on to a higher one.
Soon she reached where the little king
was stuck in the tree. The hem of his
purple robe was caught around a twig
and his crown had slipped down over
one eye. He was holding on tightly
to a branch with one hand. Under his

other arm was the Secret Spellbook, an old leather-bound book that contained powerful and ancient magic spells.

"Oh dearie me," King Merry said again in a wobbly voice. "I've never been much good at tree climbing."

Jasmine took the Secret Spellbook and carefully helped the little king to hop from branch to branch. Soon they were both on the ground.

"Thank you," he said.

Ellie brushed a few leaves from his robe while Summer rescued a ladybird from the top of his crown.

"Has something happened to Trixi?" Jasmine asked anxiously.

King Merry's face fell. "Have you girls seen her?"

The girls looked at one another in

dismay. "No, we haven't seen her since the Pet Show Spectacular," Summer told him. "Isn't she in the Secret Kingdom?"

"I don't know," King Merry sighed.

"No one's seen her for ages. I suppose I had better start at the beginning," he said, taking a deep breath. "You see, I'm going to award the Twinkle Trophy to Florence, a very special

fairy, for bringing so much magical fun
to the Secret Kingdom with her Fairy
Fairground."

"That's good," said Ellie. "Florence
will be able to break Queen Malice's
friendship bracelet spell and give Trixi
back her talent for magic!"

"But I can't present the trophy to
Florence until Trixi returns," the little
king said, wringing his hands anxiously.
"If she's not there when I do, we won't
be able to restore her stolen talent." He
looked at the girls hopefully. "Please will
you come back to the Secret Kingdom
and help me find her?"

"Of course we will!" the girls cried
together.

King Merry sighed with relief. "Let's
go right away!" He picked up the Secret

Spellbook and began to flick through the pages. "Now where did I see that travelling spell…" he mumbled to himself.

The girls gathered round to help him find it. They didn't want him to use the wrong spell and send them to Thunder Castle by mistake!

"There!" said Summer, pointing to one of the pages. "That spell should take us to the Fairy Fairground."

"Perfect," said King Merry. "Are you all ready?"

The girls quickly held hands. "Yes!" they cried.

King Merry chanted the spell:

"Ancient magic, hear our cry,
To the Fairy Fairground we must fly."

A whirlwind of colourful sparkles rose up out of the Secret Spellbook. It twirled around the girls and King Merry, lifting them off their feet.

"Secret Kingdom, here we come!" Summer cried.

They landed a few seconds later on something soft and squishy, and as the sparkles cleared they saw that they were standing on a pink bouncy castle.

"It looks like the Enchanted Palace, Your Majesty!" Ellie giggled.

"Just bouncier!" Jasmine laughed. As she jumped she felt something bouncing on her head. She put up her hand and smiled as she felt her tiara resting on her hair. Whenever they went to the Secret Kingdom, their beautiful tiaras appeared. They showed that the girls were Very Important Friends of King Merry's.

The girls and King Merry bounced off the castle and looked around.

Tiny fairies in glittering dresses flitted everywhere, waving their wands and sending spells that looked like ribbons of sparkly rainbow whizzing all about.

"It looks like we still have time to find Trixi before the fairground opens," King Merry said, nodding his head determinedly. "There's Florence," he said, pointing to a beautiful fairy with

shimmering wings. She was hovering
beside a sweet stall, where magical toffee
apples floated in the air beside
her. "Come along, let me
introduce you."
King Merry
led the way
across the
fairground,
weaving
between a
rollercoaster
shaped like a
dream dragon,
a floating teacup
ride and a carousel
where real unicorns stood
patiently, ready for people to arrive.
The girls looked round at the fairies

flying busily back and forth, hanging sparkling bunting and doing last-minute checks on the rides, laughing and joking with one another. Everyone at the fairground was so excited, but the girls knew they had to find Trixi before they could join in the fun.

Suddenly King Merry stopped and scratched his head. "Oh dear," he said. "I seem to have lost my way."

"Your Majesty," called a tinkling voice. "Over here!"

Looking round, the girls saw Florence flying towards them, her glittering wings fluttering. She was a tiny bit taller than Trixi, and she was dressed like a circus ringmaster in a sparkly red jacket and a stripy red-and-black skirt. "Welcome to the Fairy Fairground," she said, her blue eyes twinkling.

"This is
Florence," King
Merry introduced
her to Jasmine,
Summer and Ellie.

Florence smiled
at the girls. "I'm very
pleased to meet you," she
said. She flapped her wings
and performed a curtsey in
mid-air. "And I'm so excited
to see you, Your Majesty," she said.
"I can hardly wait to receive the
Twinkle Trophy and help your royal
pixie to recover her magic. It's such an
honour."

"Have you seen Trixi?" asked Jasmine.

"Not yet," the fairy replied, looking at

them all expectantly. "Why?"

The girls and King Merry exchanged anxious looks.

"Um, well. Er, the thing is, Florence…" began King Merry.

"Trixi's missing," Summer finished.

Jasmine nodded. "We have to find her, or King Merry won't be able to award the trophy."

Florence's eyes widened. "Oh dear!" she gasped. "I wonder where Trixi can be?"

Roll up!

"We've looked everywhere," King Merry said miserably. "My butlers have searched my palace from top to bottom. They've asked all of Trixi's friends if they've seen her. And two elves travelled to the Heart Tree to ask her family back home if she'd been there." He sighed heavily. "I'm really very worried about her. The Other Realm was my last hope, but she wasn't there either."

"She might arrive here when the fair opens?" Summer said hopefully.

Florence's hand flew to her mouth. "My goodness, yes! Everything's ready – we must open the fair. Hearing about poor Trixi's disappearance nearly made me forget."

They hurried to the gate with Florence flying just ahead of them, her wings twinkling with rainbow colours in the sunshine. There was already a huge

queue outside the gates, and the girls
saw brownies, pixies, elves, imps and
lots of other wonderful creatures waiting
to come in, chattering and laughing
excitedly.

"Maybe Trixi's lining up with everyone
else?" said Ellie.

They looked carefully at all the pixies
hovering on their leaves, hoping that one
of them might be their missing friend, but
she wasn't there.

King Merry climbed on to a low stage
ready to make his opening speech. He
put down the Secret Spellbook and
frowned nervously. "I wish Trixi was
here. She always knows what I should
say on these occasions," he said.

"You could just keep it simple, and
tell everyone to have a good time, Your
Majesty?" suggested Jasmine.

The king brightened up. "Yes, of
course. That would be perfect."

Florence fluttered over. "Are you
ready?" she asked.

King Merry nodded.

"Would you mind opening the gates,
please, girls?" said Florence.

Summer, Ellie and Jasmine ran to open
the gates. As they threw them wide,
beautiful music began to play.

"Roll up, roll up!" called Florence. "Roll up for lots of magical fun in the Fairy Fairground!"

The crowd gathered around the stage and the girls quickly ran back to be near King Merry. They had a feeling he might need them.

King Merry cleared his throat and swallowed nervously. "Friends," he said, "I want to welcome you all to the Hairy Hatband. No, the Bendy Bandstand. No, that's wrong, too."

"The Fairy Fairground," whispered Ellie, trying not to laugh.

"That's it! The Fairy Fairground," said King Merry. "I hope you have lots of magical fun. I hereby declare the fairground officially open!"

As he finished speaking, all the rides began to move, and music started playing loudly. The crowd cheered and a few young brownies threw their hats into the air, then everyone skipped off to look at all the stalls and rides.

"Shall I show you round?" asked Florence.

"Yes, please!" the girls chorused. They could hardly wait to see all the magical attractions.

"And we can search for Trixi as we go," added Summer.

"While we look for her, might you allow me to make the Secret Spellbook smaller for you, Your Majesty?" Florence suggested, as King Merry picked it up.

"That's a good idea," he replied. "Carrying it for too long makes my arms ache."

Florence quickly recited a spell, and sparkles fizzed around the heavy book.

Suddenly it began to shrink.

"That's perfect," said King Merry, when the book was small enough to fit in the pocket of his purple robe. "Thank you, my dear!"

King Merry and the girls followed the beautiful fairy past an enormous Ferris wheel that showered everyone

with colourful glitter as they passed by. Imps, brownies and elves were riding the unicorns on the carousel, and the dream-dragon rollercoaster was whizzing along its track, its cars filled with smiling youngsters. The fairground was packed, but there was no sign of their pixie friend.

"There's a hoopla stall," said Ellie. "How funny that we were playing that in our world earlier on."

"It's a bit different here, though," Summer giggled, stopping to watch a group of pixies trying to throw hoops over cute white rabbits who sat very still with their ears pricked up. When someone looped one of rabbits, it would hop over and give the winner their prize.

"And there's a helter-skelter," said

Jasmine. It was painted with a swirl
of red and white and a colourful flag
fluttered on the top. Two imps came
whizzing out of the bottom on a
patterned mat.

"Would you like another go?" asked a
fairy who was hovering nearby.

"Yes, please!" the imps cried eagerly.

"Jump on the mat, then!" the fairy said
with a smile, then waved her hand above
their heads and twinkling glitter settled
on the mat. "Hold tight," she added as it
rose into the air and flew them to the top
of the tower again.

"Wow, a helter-skelter and a magic
carpet rolled into one!" Jasmine said. "I
definitely want a go on that when we've
found Trixi."

"I hope we find her soon…" Summer

said. She was starting to feel worried
about their pixie friend. It felt so odd
being in the Secret Kingdom without her,
and she knew Trixi would want to share
all the fun of the Fairy Fairground.

The girls heard a toot
behind them and a train
chuffed past. A stream of
shiny, silvery bubbles poured
out of its funnel. The
carriages were packed
with pixies and elves, who

waved cheerfully as they went along.

"I shall have a ride on that," said King Merry. He looked hopefully at Florence. "I don't suppose I could drive it, could I, once we've found Trixi?"

"I don't see why not, Your Majesty," Florence replied with a smile.

"This is a wonderful fairground, Florence," said Ellie. "Everyone's having so much amazing magical fun! If only we could find Trixi—"

She was cut short, as suddenly lightning fizzed across the sky and thunder cracked loudly.

"Oh no!" gasped Summer.

"Oh yes!" cried a mean voice.

A horrible screeching noise rang out as the Ferris wheel ground to a halt. There, standing at the very top of the wheel,

was Queen Malice! She
was tall and thin and
dressed all in black.
Her wild, frizzy
black hair was
topped with a
spiky black crown.
She waved her
thunder staff and
a thundercloud
appeared to
carry her down
to the ground.

"Nobody
will have any
more fun!" she
shouted nastily as
she landed in front of them. "And Trixi
will never get her talent for magic back!"

"Yes, she will," Jasmine said bravely.

"She won't, because you'll never find her!" jeered Queen Malice.

"Where is she?" gasped Summer.

"What have you done with her?" Ellie shouted angrily.

"I've trapped her." The wicked queen gave a cruel smile. "She's right here, in a hiding place that's staring you in the face!" The mean queen threw back her head and cackled shrilly. Then she turned to King Merry with a sly smile. "Of course, brother, you can have your precious royal pixie back right now if you give me your crown. I'd be a much better ruler than you, after all."

"Very well, Malice," King Merry said, sighing heavily. He reached up to take off his crown, but Summer, Ellie and

Jasmine all called out to him.

"No, Your Majesty!" they shouted.

"We'll find Trixi. There's no way she'd want you to give your crown to your nasty sister!" Summer said determinedly.

Jasmine nodded. "We can't give in!"

Queen Malice laughed again. "In that case, your pixie pal can say goodbye to her magic. Talent Week is almost at an end, and Trixi will stay missing until it's over." She smiled nastily. "So whether you award Florence the Twinkle Trophy now, or wait until the last second of Talent Week, your precious pixie will *never* get her magic back!"

Searching for Trixi

The girls looked at each other in horror.
"Poor Trixi!" cried Ellie.

"You won't stop me this time!" sneered
Queen Malice. She raised her hands and
seven of her horrid Storm Sprite servants
came swooping down and landed
around her. "Wreck everything!" she
commanded. "Make sure that nobody
has any more fun!" She banged down

her thunderbolt staff and another black storm cloud appeared beneath her feet. It floated up into the sky, taking the mean queen with it.

The Storm Sprites spread their bat-like wings and took off again. Squawking with laughter, they ripped the flag from the roof of the helter-skelter and pushed it into the train's bubble funnel. The train stopped suddenly, jolting everybody inside. Some young elves began to cry, and the Storm Sprites laughed unkindly. "No more silly rides for you!" one of them jeered.

More Storm Sprites appeared in the air above the girls. They were carrying large drops of silvery water. "They've got Misery Drops!" Ellie groaned. "Where are they going with those?"

Nudging each other and
laughing gleefully,
the Storm Sprites
flew to the
floating teacup
ride. "Do you
want some
Misery Drops in
your tea?" one
called.

The Storm
Sprites let the
Misery Drops
fall, and the
young fairies,
brownies and
imps scrambled
out of the giant
teacups just in time.

"We've got to stop them!" gasped Summer. The girls followed the sprites over to the dream-dragon rollercoaster, where they started pulling faces at the young riders.

"Leave them alone!" shouted Jasmine bravely.

But the Storm Sprites took no notice, flying over to the unicorn carousel.

"Bombs away!" they yelled.

"Look out, everyone!" shouted Ellie, as the Misery Drops sped towards the ground.

All the riders jumped off the unicorns and ran clear, but the unicorns on the carousel couldn't get out of the way in time. The Misery Drops hit them and magically changed their mood. Instead of smiling happily, their heads and tails drooped and they looked terribly sad.

"This is terrible!" Florence gasped, looking around at the fairground in dismay, as more Storm Sprites smashed a magical cake-and-candyfloss stand. "My fairies and I have spent weeks magically creating this fairground so everyone could have fun. And now it's ruined!"

"We'll help put things right," Summer told her. "And when we find Trixi and she gets her magic back, she'll help too."

"We have to keep looking for her," said Jasmine. "Queen Malice said she'd hidden Trixi in a place that was staring us in the face. What do you think she mean by that?"

They all thought hard, but they couldn't work it out.

"Let's keep searching while we're thinking," Ellie suggested.

"But there are so many places to look," said Summer. "And Trixi's so tiny. She could be anywhere."

"That's very true," King Merry agreed in a worried voice. "Poor Trixi."

"Why don't we get more people to help?" Jasmine suggested. "If more of us

are looking, we should find her quickly."
She raised her voice. "We need helpers,
please!"

A group of elves looked up from one of
the wrecked rides.

"Over here!" cried Florence.

The elves ran over, calling to their
friends, and soon quite a large crowd of
brownies, elves, pixies and fairies had
gathered.

"We need to find King Merry's
royal pixie, Trixi," said Ellie. "Queen
Malice has captured her and hidden her
somewhere in the fairground. Will you
please help us look for her?"

"Of course we will," said a gnome
wearing a purple hat.

The girls divided everyone into four
teams. "Each team can search a quarter

of the fairground," Jasmine said.

"We'll look near the entrance," said
Summer. "This way, everyone."

She led her team across the ruined
fairground, and then they spread out and
began to search, starting with the bouncy
bumper cars. Summer and her helpers
looked inside every overturned car. There
was no sign of Trixi, so they moved on
to the dream-dragon rollercoaster.

"Search everywhere you can," Jasmine said to her team. The fairies fluttered all around the helter-skelter, while Jasmine and some elves searched the wreckage of the hoopla stall and two cake-and-candyfloss stands. But Trixi was nowhere to be found.

Florence led her team of searchers to the east side of the fairground.

King Merry joined Ellie's team as they searched the west. "I hope we find Trixi soon," he said sadly as they searched the bubble train. "I miss her dreadfully."

"We all do, but we'll find her," said Ellie reassuringly.

They searched the train from top to bottom and the smallest fairies even flew underneath all the carriages, but Trixi wasn't there.

The girls, King Merry, Florence and their search teams all met up again by the unicorn carousel.

"We've looked everywhere," sighed Summer. "Where can Trixi be?"

The girls exchanged desperate looks. They couldn't bear to think of their friend being trapped somewhere.

"Wait!" Summer said suddenly, lowering her voice and glancing overhead as some more Storm Sprites flew above them. "I think I have an idea…"

The Hall of Misty Mirrors

Summer looked around the group.
"Perhaps we can find out where Trixi is
from the Storm Sprites?" she said.

Ellie looked puzzled. "I don't think the
Storm Sprites will tell us anything…"

"No, but if we follow them they might
lead us to Trixi!" Summer said cheerfully.

"Oh yes!" said Jasmine.

"That's a great idea!" Ellie exclaimed.

"King Merry and I will look over here," Florence suggested.

"We'll go this way," Jasmine said. "I think I saw some sprites over by the fit fairy machine."

Summer, Ellie and Jasmine hid out of sight and watched as one of the sprites snatched up the big wooden mallet and whacked a pad at the base of the machine. A dinger flew up and hit a bell at the top and beautiful fairy music began to play.

"Let me have a go, big

nose!" shouted the other Storm Sprite. He seized the mallet and banged it down on the pad.

The dinger shot up again, ringing the bell and setting the music playing more loudly than ever.

"Give that here!" the first Storm Sprite shouted, snatching the mallet back.

"No, I want it!" cried the other.

They went on squabbling, and bashing the mallet down hard. The bell rang out again and again and the music grew louder and more unpleasant.

"They're breaking it," Ellie whispered, frowning, but the others held their fingers to their lips.

"Let's just see where they go next," Jasmine said quietly.

"Where else can we cause trouble?"

one of the Storm Sprites was asking another.

"Anywhere except the hall of misty mirrors," the other replied. "Queen Malice said we weren't allowed to go there."

"Why can't they go there?" whispered Ellie. "Unless…" She looked excitedly at Summer and Jasmine. "Hang on a minute! Queen Malice said Trixi's hiding place would be staring us in the face – like a mirror!"

"Of course," Jasmine said eagerly. "The hall of misty mirrors must be where she's trapped Trixi!"

"Let's find King Merry and Florence!" cried Summer.

The girls raced through the fairground, looking left and right as they ran. At last they found King Merry. He was creeping along behind a group of Storm Sprites wearing a pair of sunglasses. His collar was turned up and his crown pulled down low over his forehead.

"I think he's trying to look like a spy," Jasmine whispered, trying not to giggle.

They tapped the little king on the shoulder, and he spun round so quickly that his sunglasses fell off. "Oh! Hello, girls! Have you found Trixi?" he asked hopefully.

"We think she's in the hall of misty mirrors," said Summer quickly. She picked up his sunglasses, but King Merry waved them away and took his own half-moon glasses out of his pocket.

"I think I prefer these," he said.

"The hall of misty mirrors is very close," Florence said, fluttering over to them. "Just behind the carousel." She pointed to a long low building with sparkly lilac walls.

They dashed over to it, raced inside and found themselves in a maze of mirrors with many mist-cloaked paths that twisted and turned in all directions.

"Trixi!" King Merry called.

"Are you in here? Trixi?" Summer shouted, and the others joined in.

"Trixi! Trixi! Are you here?"

But then suddenly Jasmine spotted something.

"Look! Over here!" she cried, seeing the pixie's tiny face peeping out from one of the mirrors. Trixi seemed to be looking over Jasmine's shoulder.

"She's here!" Jasmine cried. "I've found Trixi!" She whirled round eagerly, expecting to see Trixi right behind her, but there was nothing but glittering mist and more mirrors there.

Puzzled, Jasmine turned back to the mirror. Trixi's reflection was still there above her shoulder, grinning delightedly, but then mist swirled across it, blotting it out. By the time Ellie and Summer reached Jasmine, the mist was clearing again.

"There!" said Jasmine, pointing to

the mirror. But Trixi had vanished
once more, and so had Jasmine's *own*
reflection, even though she was standing
only a few centimetres from the glass!

"How confusing! What's happening?"
Jasmine said to the others, bewildered.
"I definitely thought I saw Trixi a
moment ago."

Just then, Trixi's voice rang out: "Girls! King Merry! I'm here!"

"Trixi!" gasped Summer, calling out to their friend. "Are you all right? Where are you?"

"Over here!"

They all turned and saw Trixi, hovering on her leaf, smiling and waving at them.

"Oh, thank goodness!" King Merry cried. They all rushed towards Trixi, but as they got closer, her reflection changed – into a sneering Storm Sprite!

The Middle of the Maze

The girls, King Merry and Florence all came to a halt, frowning in confusion.

"You nasty Storm Sprite, tell us where Trixi is this instant!" King Merry shouted, but the sprite in the mirror just vanished, the sound of his cackling laughter echoing around the hall.

"I'm here!" they heard Trixi cry once more. "But Queen Malice has put a spell on the mirrors!"

The girls looked at each other in horror. How would they ever find their pixie friend now?

"We're going to try and look for you, Trixi," called Summer, her voice trembling a little with worry.

The girls, King Merry and Florence rushed through the maze-like hall of mirrors, setting the glittering mist swirling. Everywhere they looked they saw reflections, but they kept appearing and disappearing.

"If only I could take away Queen
Malice's spell," sighed Florence as she
fluttered overhead, "but her magic is
much stronger than mine."

"I can see Trixi!"
called Ellie, but it
quickly changed
to Jasmine's
face in the
mirror,
and then
to the face
of another
grinning Storm
Sprite.

"I can see her, too,"
Jasmine shouted. "Oh, she's gone again."
She hurried on through the maze, but
she was beginning to feel panicky. How

could they tell which reflections were
real and which were created by Queen
Malice's mean spell?

"I'm over here," Trixi called once
more, her voice echoing sadly.

Everyone turned towards the sound of
her voice, but there was no sign of her
in the mirrors. All the girls, King Merry
and Florence could see were their own
reflections.

"Ha ha!" A sniggering noise filled the
hall as a group of Storm Sprites swooped
along the corridor and began flying
around them, blowing raspberries.

"You'll never find your precious pixie!"
one of them taunted.

"All you're going to see in these mirrors
is us!" another said, cackling loudly.

Florence fluttered up toward the Storm

Sprites with her hands on her hips, frowning. "Leave us alone!" she said.

She looked down at the girls and King Merry, and winked. "My magic might not be strong enough to break Queen Malice's spell, but at least I can take care of these sprites!"

She waved her hand and magical glitter fluttered down onto each of the Storm Sprites. All at once they began to sneeze, over and over again.

"ACHOO! Achoo!" they sneezed.

"Let's – ACHOO! – get out of here!"
one called, and they all flapped out of
the maze.

"Well done, Florence!" King Merry
cheered. "Now, we must find Trixi
before it's too late…"

Jasmine looked around desperately, and
tried calling out again. "Where are you,
Trixi?" she said. "We can't see you!"

"I'm over here," Trixi said sadly.

The girls looked at each other as Trixi's
voice echoed around.

Then Ellie clapped her hands. "I've had
an idea!" she said excitedly. "We can't
see the real Trixi, but we *can* hear her."

Summer grinned. "Of course! If we shut
our eyes so we can't see any reflections,
we can follow the sound of Trixi's voice
until we find her!"

"That's a great idea," Jasmine said. "Trixi, why don't you sing a song for us to follow?"

"OK," Trixi called. Suddenly the room was filled with the sound of her sweet pixie voice.

The girls closed their eyes tight. Stretching their arms out in front of them, so they wouldn't bump into the mirrored walls, they shuffled forward, listening carefully.

King Merry and Florence did the same.

"Keep singing, Trixi!" Ellie said, feeling her way along the cool glass and squeezing her eyes more tightly shut.

"I think her song's getting louder," said Summer. "We must be close!"

After feeling their way through the maze for a few more minutes, at last they reached the middle and they heard Trixi stop singing suddenly.

"I can see you all!" she cried excitedly.

They all opened their eyes, and there was a tiny mirrored box.

Ellie stepped forward and opened it – and Trixi flew out! She twirled around them on her flying leaf, laughing excitedly, and flew up to kiss each of them on the nose. The girls giggled at her celebration.

"Oh, it's so wonderful to be free again!" Trixi said.

"Are you OK?" asked Jasmine.

"I am now," the little pixie replied happily.

"We'd better get out of here," Ellie said, "before Queen Malice's magic confuses us again."

They all rushed out of the hall of misty mirrors and into the fresh air.

"Thanks for rescuing me," Trixi said, grinning. "A group of elves came in searching for me earlier, but the mixed-up reflections confused them and they were talking so loudly that they couldn't hear me calling out to them."

Summer turned to King Merry. "Can you award the Twinkle Trophy to Florence straightaway, Your Majesty?" she asked.

"Good idea," said Florence. "Then I can restore Trixi's talent for magic and we can put the Fairy Fairground right!"

Trixi's face suddenly fell and she burst into tears.

"Oh Trixi, what's wrong?" kind-hearted Summer cried.

"I was so pleased to see you all that
I forgot to tell you," Trixi sobbed,
"Queen Malice took my pixie ring!"
The pixie held out her hand sadly.
"Even if Florence uses the Twinkle
Trophy award, I can't get my magic
back without it. Queen Malice hid it in
amongst the prizes in the candy-crab
grabber."

The girls exchanged anxious looks. The
sun was already sinking and night was
starting to darken the eastern edge of the
sky. Today was the last day of Talent
Week and it would very soon be over.
If Trixi didn't get her magic back by
nightfall it would be lost forever!

The Candy-Crab Grabber

"The candy-crab grabber is this way! Come on, let's find that ring!" Florence said, flying away as fast as her wings would carry her.

The girls, King Merry and Trixi raced after her to a large grassy area in the corner of the fairground. It was filled with sparkly slot machines that played tunes and gave off puffs of glittering

smoke and swirls of colour when the
brownies, elves and imps playing them
won prizes. The candy-crab grabber
was right at the back. "It looks as
though this is the one bit that the Storm
Sprites haven't wrecked," said Florence,
breathing a sigh of relief. "It's lovely to
see everyone enjoying themselves."

Suddenly a Storm Sprite swooped low
over their heads. He landed beside them.

The candy-crab grabber was a large
glass box filled with sparkly baubles,
each with a toy inside. Right in the
middle, on a spinning platform, sat a
pink-and-white candy-striped crab with
glittering silver pincers. As the watched,
a little elf girl stepped forward and picked
up the controller, turning the crab so
that he could reach the prize she wanted

with one of his claws.

"That one, please," she said, pointing at a shiny blue bauble.

But before the crab could reach it, a Storm Sprite grabbed hold of the controller, spinning the crab around wildly.

"I want a go!" the sprite yelled.

"It's my turn!" said the little girl firmly.
She held on to the controller while the
nasty Storm Sprite tried to wrestle it
away from her. The crab spun back and
forth as they fought.

King Merry hurried over to them.
"Go away," he said sternly to the Storm
Sprite. "You've caused quite enough
trouble for one day."

"Unless you want to start sneezing
again," Florence warned the sprite.

The Storm Sprite stuck his tongue out
at them, then he spread his leathery
wings and flew up into the air and away.

"Thank goodness he's gone," said
Summer with a shudder.

Ellie hurried to speak to the little elf
girl. "We need to look for something
very important inside the candy-crab

grabber," she said. "Do you mind if we search for it, please?"

The little elf girl stared at their tiaras in amazement, then nodded.

Jasmine, Summer, Ellie and King Merry all crowded round and peered inside the glass case. Florence and Trixi flew above their heads for a better view. The crab waved his claws dizzily.

"That was horrible," he grumbled. "No more prizes today."

Trixi gasped.

"Oh please, Mr Crab," Summer stepped forward and spoke to him gently. "We're sorry the sprite made you dizzy, but we really need your help."

The crab wriggled his stripy claws thoughtfully.

Jasmine was looking at the baubles

through the glass case. She guessed that
Trixi's ring was hidden in one of them,
but it was impossible to see what was
inside them. How would they ever find
the right one?

"OK," the crab said finally. "Which
one do you want? How about that one?"
he asked helpfully. "Or that one over
there?"

"This is going to take too long," Ellie
whispered, not wanting to be rude to the
crab. "We'll have to look inside all of
them – and quickly!"

Summer smiled at the crab. "I know
you usually chose one at a time, but can
I ask you to do something special for
us? Please will you drop all the balls out
through the slot, so we can find Trixi
the Royal Pixie's missing ring? Please,

it's really important. And then you don't have to do any more today."

"Humph. I suppose so," the crab said grumpily.

"Thank goodness you've got your talent for befriending animals back," Jasmine said, squeezing Summer's hand.

The crab began to grab the baubles.

He dropped them out through the slot where they floated upwards and bobbed in mid-air, sending out rays of coloured light. The children in the queue came crowding round.

"Can we help?" one of them asked.

"Yes! We need to open all the baubles," said Jasmine. "But we've got to do it carefully because we're looking

for a really tiny pixie ring."

Eagerly everyone picked a bauble out of the air and unscrewed it. They all contained toys – tiny teddies, dolls, skipping ropes and skittle sets that grew full-sized the moment they were lifted out of their little containers.

More children came to help, but the

crab was working furiously, and more and more baubles were floating around the machine. Glancing up, Ellie saw that darkness was stealing across the sky. Her heart began to pound. Would they find Trixi's ring before Talent Week was over?

"We have to hurry!" gasped Florence. "It's nearly dark."

"I've found something glittery!" the little elf girl from earlier called, holding up an open bauble with something tiny shimmering inside.

The girls watched anxiously as Trixi

swooped over to her on her leaf.

"It's my pixie ring!" she whooped.
"You've found it!"

The Last Talent Week Award

Trixi slid the ring on to her finger, then twirled her leaf in the air in delight. "Thanks for your help," she called to the children. "And thank you!" she said to the crab, blowing him a kiss.

The crab blushed completely pink. "You're welcome!" he said gruffly.

"Quickly, King Merry," cried Jasmine.

There was just a thin line of daylight left along one edge of the sky. "Can you give Florence the Twinkle Trophy right now please?"

The king began to feel in his pockets. "I know it's here somewhere," he said. "It's very small, of course, because Florence's not that big…"

"Try your waistcoat pocket, Your Majesty!" cried Trixi. "That's where you keep most of your important things."

King Merry plunged his hand into his waistcoat pocket and pulled out a tiny silver trophy that twinkled in the light. "Here it is!" he gasped. "Thank goodness you're back, Trixi!" He turned to Florence. "You, Florence, have won this award for bringing magical fun to the Secret Kingdom." He handed it to

her and she held it
above her head.
Glitter dust
showered
down on her,
making her
hair shimmer
with silver
light.

Now the
girls noticed that
a large crowd had
gathered to watch the ceremony. They
began to cheer and clap.

Florence held up her hand for quiet.
"I am very proud to win this wonderful
award, and most of all, to share the extra
powers it has given me with Trixi, so
that she can perform magic again!"

Florence flew up into the air and held the trophy to the dull black metal of the little pixie's cursed bracelet. More glitter dust showered down, surrounding Trixi with a rosy pink glow. There was a loud crack, and the bracelet changed back to the lovely shade of green it had been when Trixi first put it on, with a beautiful leaf charm hanging from it. Trixi grinned as her pixie ring began to twinkle so

brightly that the girls had to shade their
eyes.

"Here goes," Trixi said nervously.
"Time to see if it's really worked."

Ellie squeezed Jasmine's and Summer's
hands as they waited anxiously to see
what would happen.

Trixi turned towards the bouncy
bumper cars, which were still lying
on their sides. Tapping her ring, she
chanted:

"Let magic sparkles pour like rain
And stand up all those cars again."

Rainbow coloured sparkles whooshed
out of the ring in a glittering fountain.
They swirled around the bumper cars,
lifting them high, then setting them down

again the right way up.

"It's worked!"
cried Jasmine,
dancing an
excited jig
on the spot.

"Well
done, Trixi!
Well done,
Florence!"
exclaimed
Summer.

"And only just
in time," Ellie added
breathlessly, looking at the darkening
sky. "Talent Week is over."

Smiling delightedly, Trixi flew high on
her leaf, and then spiralled back to them
all. "Thank goodness!" she cried. "I've

got my magic back at last!"

The crowd began to cheer again, then King Merry took the Secret Spellbook out of his pocket. At once it grew back to its normal size. "We must fix the Fairy Fairground," he said, as the cheers died away.

"Will everyone please help us put right the Storm Sprites' damage?" Florence called.

Trixi tapped her ring, and all the other fairies and pixies started using their magic too. The girls hurried through the fairground, watching the colourful spells fizz and sparkle against the night sky as the broken rides and stalls were repaired.

"It's better than a firework display!" Ellie exclaimed.

But before the girls could celebrate,

there was a rumble of thunder and
lightning flashed across the sky. Suddenly
rain poured down,
and Queen Malice
appeared,
splashing
though the
puddles. Her
Storm Sprites
were clustered
around her and
they grinned
nastily at all
the creatures
running for
shelter from the
storm.

"Yet again, you have ruined my
plans!" the mean queen screeched over

the sound of the rain.

The girls exchanged anxious looks. It would be terrible if Queen Malice and her Storm Sprites ruined the fairground again!

"Well, this time you won't win!" she continued. She raised her thunderbolt staff, but before she could bang it down, Trixi flew in front of the girls. "Leave this to me!" she cried, even though huge raindrops were shaking her leaf. "Queen Malice has picked the wrong day to try and spoil things. There's a whole week's worth of magic in my pixie ring that I haven't been able to use. And Florence's Twinkle Trophy dust has made it stronger than ever!"

Ignoring the queen's scowl, she tapped her ring and chanted:

"Queen Malice loves to stop our fun
So let her think about what she's done!"

A huge whirlwind of pink sparkles
zoomed out of her ring. Queen Malice
and the Storm Sprites
tried to dodge them,
but the sparkles
twirled around
them and lifted
all of them off
their feet.

"Put us
down!"
shrieked
the queen.
She tried
to point her
staff at Trixi,

but the sparkles spun her away to the happy house and dropped her down the chimney, with the Storm Sprites tumbling after her.

Trixi tapped her pixie ring again and the rain stopped. The storm clouds started to melt away, leaving a bright blue sky behind.

"What will happen to them in the happy house, Trixi?" asked Summer.

The little pixie grinned. "Lots of elf tickles and jokes," she said. "And they won't be able to leave until the clock strikes midnight. And while they're stuck, we can finally have some fun in the Fairy Fairground!"

"Yes, please!" the girls cried together.

"Let's try the helter-skelter first," said Jasmine eagerly.

It was very late by the time the girls had been on every ride. The sky was a deep bluey-black and stars twinkled brightly. "Thank you for all your help," Florence said happily.

"We've had an amazing time," said Ellie with a happy sigh. "The bouncy bumper cars are brilliant."

"So's the helter-skelter and magic carpet ride," said Jasmine.

"And the carousel," Summer added. "There's nothing nicer than a ride on a unicorn!"

A toot sounded behind them and they turned to see what it was. King Merry was driving the train! He was wearing a train driver's cap underneath his crown and he was grinning from ear to ear.

"I've asked Florence if she'll magic me a train for the garden of the Enchanted Palace," he called. "This is the best fun I've had in ages!"

The train chugged past and the girls held hands. Trixi beamed at them.

"I've enjoyed the fairground, too," she said, "but getting my magic back is the best thing of all. Thank you for your help."

"We'll always do whatever we can to help our friends in the Secret Kingdom," said Jasmine, glancing down at her friendship bracelet. "In fact," she said, "I'm going to keep wearing my bracelet, to remind me of all my friends here."

"Me too." Summer grinned.

"Queen Malice gave us a nice gift after all!" Ellie said, laughing.

Trixi smiled as she looked at her bracelet. "I'll wear it always to remind me of you," she said. "But for now, I think it's time you were getting home."

The girls nodded and joined hands.

Trixi tapped her pixie ring. A cloud of pink sparkles flooded out and surrounded them.

"Goodbye!" they called as they were lifted off their feet. A moment later they landed with a gentle bump. It was broad daylight and they were back behind the tree near the magician's tent at the Honeyvale County Fair.

"What an amazing day!" exclaimed Ellie. "Those magical rides were brilliant! And since no time has passed, we've still got the whole day here at the fete!"

"I wonder what adventure we'll have next time we go to the Secret Kingdom," said Summer.

"I don't know, but I'm sure it'll be a good one," said Jasmine. "And at least we have our talents back. We'll be able to stop Queen Malice no matter what she does next."

Ellie and Summer hugged her.

"With the help of our friends in the Secret Kingdom," Ellie said with a smile, "We can do anything!"

In the next Secret Kingdom adventure, Ellie, Summer and Jasmine join their friends at the

Petal Parade

Read on for a sneak peek...

A Garden Riddle

Butterflies danced from flower to flower in the sunshine and birds sang in the trees. It was a beautiful summer day and Jasmine Smith was helping her grandmother – Nani – in their garden. Best of all, her two best friends, Summer Hammond and Ellie Macdonald, were helping, too. Nani, who lived with

Jasmine and her mum, was trimming some roses while the girls planted flowers in pots.

"I love gardening!" said Summer, pushing her blonde plaits back over her shoulder as she watched a ladybird walk across the top of the pot she was planting.

"Me too," said Jasmine. "I love the smell of the flowers and the earth."

Ellie had taken a little break from planting and was drawing one of Nani's garden gnomes in her sketchbook. Each of the little plastic gnomes dotted around the garden had a red hat, white beard and rosy cheeks. Some were fishing, others were sweeping or pushing wheelbarrows. "These gnomes are so cute," Ellie said. She grinned and picked up the one she was drawing. "You know what he's saying?" she asked the others.

"What?" asked Summer.

"There's no place like gnome!"

Summer and Jasmine giggled.

Jasmine dusted her gloves off. "Why don't you tell the plants a story, Summer? It might help them to grow."

Nani chuckled as she walked past them with a watering can. "I'm not sure stories help plants grow," she said. "What they need is sunshine and water, and what you girls need is your lunch. Why don't I go and get some food ready while you finish off here?"

"Thanks, Nani," said Jasmine as her grandmother went inside.

"I know Nani says that plants don't need stories to grow," Ellie whispered, "but they do in the Secret Kingdom!"

The three girls all shared a smile. They had an amazing secret. They looked after a Magic Box that could whisk them away to a magical land called the Secret Kingdom. All sorts of wonderful creatures like mermaids and unicorns, elves and brownies lived there, ruled by a jolly king named King Merry.

"Do you remember the time we went to Fairytale Forest?" asked Summer. "And saw books growing on trees!"

Jasmine nodded. "It was brilliant!"

"Oh, I do love the Secret Kingdom!" Ellie said, her green eyes shining. "I hope we go there again soon. It's been ages since King Merry last asked us to visit."

"We could look at the Magic Box now and see if there's a message for us," said Summer hopefully.

"Good idea," said Jasmine. "It's on my desk." Jasmine didn't have any nosy little brothers or sisters, so she didn't have to be as careful as Ellie and Summer when it was her turn to look after the Magic Box.

The girls ran into the house. Jasmine stuck her head into the kitchen, where her grandmother was busy getting their lunch ready.

"I'm just showing the girls something in my room, Nani."

Ellie and Summer followed Jasmine into her bedroom. There was a bed with pretty netting over it and hot pink walls covered with posters of Jasmine's favourite dancers and singers. On a neat white desk sat the Magic Box, shimmering with bright light.

The girls gasped in delight.

"King Merry has sent us a message!" Ellie exclaimed.

"Quick! Let's see what it says," cried Summer.

The Magic Box had wooden sides carved with fantastic creatures and its mirrored lid was shining brightly. Words in swirly writing scrolled across the lid. Ellie read them out loud:

"The place you seek hides out of view,

There's flowers, plants and a fountain, too."

She frowned and looked at the others. "I wonder what that means."

"We need the map to solve the riddle," said Jasmine.

The lid of the box opened and a map

floated out of one of the compartments inside. It unfolded itself in front of the girls' noses. They leaned over the map eagerly and watched with delight as the pictures on it moved. There were lilac-coloured otters splashing in the sparkling waters of Sapphire Stream, fluffy snow bears tumbling through the pink snow near the Snow Bear Sanctuary, and tiny pixies swooping around the turrets of the pixie flying school. Just looking at them made Jasmine tingle with excitement. The Secret Kingdom was such an incredible place!

Read

Petal Parade

to find out what
happens next!

Secret Kingdom

Have you read all the books in Series Six?

Sparkle Statue

ROSIE BANKS

Melody Medal

ROSIE BANKS

Pet Show Prize

ROSIE BANKS

Twinkle Trophy

ROSIE BANKS

Can Summer, Jasmine, Ellie and Trixi
defeat Queen Malice and get their talents
back before Talent Week is over?

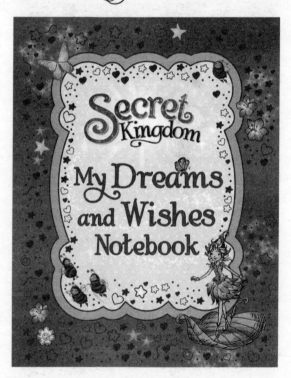

Look out for the next
sweet special!

Out now!

Trixi has lost her talent for magic!
Can you help her find all the correct words
for her spell in the word search below?

Spell:

Friendship and fun for everyone!

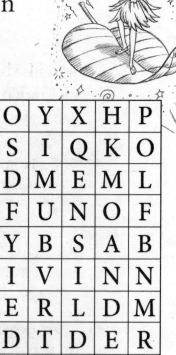

G	L	K	F	O	O	Y	X	H	P
J	Y	I	E	I	S	I	Q	K	O
I	G	I	V	P	D	M	E	M	L
B	H	C	E	L	F	U	N	O	F
E	N	A	R	D	Y	B	S	A	B
L	R	J	Y	I	I	V	I	N	N
D	U	L	O	E	E	R	L	D	M
A	H	A	N	S	D	T	D	E	R
F	R	I	E	N	D	S	H	I	P
L	I	M	T	C	S	A	E	R	H
I	M	E	S	F	O	R	N	S	O

Competition!

Would you like to win one of three Secret Kingdom goody bags?

All you have to do is design and create your own
friendship bracelet just like Ellie, Summer and Jasmine's!

Here is how to enter:

✳ Visit www.secretkingdombooks.com
✳ Click on the competition page at the top
✳ Print out the bracelet activity sheet and decorate it
✳ Once you've made your bracelet send your entry into us

The lucky winners will receive an extra special Secret Kingdom
goody bag full of treats and activities.

Please send entries to:
Secret Kingdom Friendship Bracelet Competition
Orchard Books, 338 Euston Road, London, NW1 3BH

Don't forget to add your name and address.

Good luck!

Closing dates:

There are three chances to win
before the closing date on the 30th October 2015

Secret Kingdom

A magical world of
friendship and fun!

Join the Secret Kingdom Club at

www.secretkingdombooks.com

and enjoy games, sneak peeks and lots more!

You'll find great activities, competitions, stories
and games, plus a special newsletter for
Secret Kingdom friends!